THE FIX-IT MAN

For Martyn, the original fix-it man — D.P.

For Drew, Georgia, Ebony and Beau,
the bravest family I know. — N.J.

First published 2017

EK Books
an imprint of Exisle Publishing Pty Ltd
'Moonrising', Narone Creek Road, Wollombi, NSW 2325, Australia
P.O. Box 60–490, Titirangi, Auckland 0642, New Zealand
www.ekbooks.org

A CiP record for this book is available from the National Library of
Australia.

ISBN 978-1-925335-34-7

Designed by Big Cat Design
Typeset in Sabon 18 on 24pt
Printed in China

This book uses paper sourced under ISO 14001 guidelines from
well-managed forests and other controlled sources.

10 9 8 7 6 5 4 3 2 1

paradise kids

Paradise Kids Children's Charity QLD endorses
The Fix-It Man as part of their programs to 'help heal
the heartache'. www.paradisekids.org.au

C⊙PYRIGHTAGENCY

The author gratefully acknowledges the Copyright
Agency of Australia's Creative Industries Career
Fund grant for assistance in completing this project.

www.copyright.com.au

THE FIX-IT MAN

Dimity Powell & Nicky Johnston

My dad can fix anything.

It's what dads do.

He's handy with a hammer when my
furniture falls apart. He's nifty with a needle
and thread, can untangle knots I can't.

With super glue and broken
wings, he's just amazing.
Thank goodness Dad is always
here for my 'It was an accident!'
situations.

While Dad fixes, I fetch
and Mama watches from
her rug, the one Dad
stitched together from
rainbows and old hugs.

She's too sore on the inside to help us
but her fingers still work fine. She hooks
tiny diamonds into starbursts and
snowflakes while Tiger sits close by.

Dad makes Mama's bad days
better too, with his soothing
peach and honey brew.

We make kites dance and puppets sing

until the house hums with laughter.

Tiger joins the party until ... Uh oh, disaster!

'Don't worry. I can fix it!' says Dad. 'It's what dads do.'

'Ta da! See!

Almost as good as new.'

But not Mama.

She can't be fixed by doctors or peach
and honey tea. Mama can't be fixed with
lots of rest or even by Dad ... or me.

I make us tea like Dad did.

The kitchen smells just like before …

But I can't get it right. The cracks are too wide.

And tea seeps all over the floor.

Tiger needs urgent attention.

He's too broken to dance or to sing.

We've run out of glue and I need some

more fast because sticky tape is hopeless

on bad dreams ... and teapots ...

... and Tiger.

It sounds like Dad is breaking too.
His lap is cosy and warm but his
face is crumpled and wet.

I check Dad all over for cracks and
holes, worried we'll have more to fix.

Pieces spill out from Tiger's heart
as Dad takes him from my hand.
'I can't fix him, Dad.'

He looks at me.

He looks at Tiger.

'Yes we can.'

Dad eases the rips together as I stroke Tiger's
silky head. 'It's not so bad,' Dad smiles at us.
'Now, where is my needle and thread?'

Tiger hardly hears him. But I do.

I lay my head on Dad's heart.

He squeezes tight, and I squeeze back.

No need for nails or glue.

No need for needles or thread or tea.

We can fix things together, just Dad and me.

It's what dads and daughters do.